I0713230

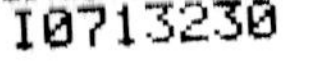

Puppers Talkin' Here . . .

Do dogs *REALLY* talk?

DEBB SNYDER

ISBN-13: 978-0-99897366-5-5

ISBN-10: 0-9987366-5-1

Wandering Stream
Literary and Publishing

email: info@wanderingstream.org

TABLE OF CONTENTS

FORWARD

PUPPERS TALKIN' HERE is an inspirational book for children and adults. Deborah "Debb" Snyder's ability to interpret Puppers' body language and capture it in this heart-warming book is a special gift for all of us to enjoy. I have witnessed the authenticity of their communication . . . and it was beautiful. I am confident that as you read, you will look forward to what Puppers will say next.

Puppers was a faithful service animal and a genuine friend to Debb. One of Puppers favorite things to do was to ride around on their "Cadillac Convertible." He loved it!

Debb and Puppers would use this time together to encourage others by saying "Jesus loves you". It was quite a ministry and they touched many lives together!

As a close friend of Debb and Puppers, it is my prayer that this small book will touch your life. May God speak to and encourage you as you read and enjoy the words written on every page.

Hats off to you, Debb, for writing such a unique book!

DONALD SULLIVAN

PREFACE

I think there are few people who *wouldn't* attribute human characteristics to their pets. We seem to see what they want by their body language and unique forms of communicating with us.

That is what I found most fascinating when I watched Puppers. He had given me many insights into not only myself, but also human behaviors.

You see, Puppers was MORE than just a pet. He was my disability service animal. It's hard to even *call* him an animal, because he acted so human.

His lack of ability to communicate in understandable English didn't make him more of an animal...it just meant I had to look more CLOSELY at his body language, facial expressions and antics to draw invaluable lessons from them.

I believe that is why I've written this book using mini-chapters. Because Puppers and I "talked" a lot over a number of years, I interpreted him into the language of a child as Puppers was "talking."

For instance, he might tip his head to the side . . . this could mean he was trying to tell me he didn't **understand.** And then I interpreted that single word into a child's language using the child's word **"unnerstand."** So, as you read the book, realize that there are NO misspellings when Puppers is talking. There can be a lot of little in-road values and morals that might be helpful not only to children, but also to adults. So I've been told from adults who have read the stories throughout the years.

So, I ask you to read on...enjoy the life of Puppers as much as Puppers and I enjoyed writing this book . . . then continue to read on and on and on . . .

MAMA DEBB AND PUPPERS

DEDICATION

To: the One who holds us when no one else will.

To: Donald Sullivan for his prayers, encouragement, and continued friendship as he helped me in managing this book project and contributing ideas.

To: Mason Campbell for his patience in teaching me computer tidbits, building me a new computer and helping me with the layout of this book.

To: Puppers for his endless love, joy and constant compassion as my little friend and for his faithful service to me.

To: Dr. Bernheimer for his compassion and care to take care of my eyes while I finished this book.

To: Dr. David Pfaff for his Christian compassion and health care for over twenty years

HE STILL REACHES OUT

The doorbell rang and my heart began pounding. I had been waiting for this moment. I opened the door wide and there he was, sitting in the hands of a man who was quite large, but gentle as could be.

He chose to put his front paws together and wave them back and forth like he was rowing a boat out of water. The man smiled and said, "Here." I was still stunned by this creature's pure black coat and his smallness. God-given joy comes in little packages with rowing paws. I tried to imagine those rowing paws and that hopeful face saying, "I want to come to you," or "Hey, how's it goin'?"

And that is how this book about Puppers and Mama Debb was born.

I picked him up even more gently than I would a baby—he was like a newborn baby and just as fragile. He curled up in my arms and began to kiss my chin like he was lapping up water.

The man said Puppers might need to go outside. I rushed him quickly to the back patio and yard. It was as if someone had wound up the tail of a toy because he literally zoomed out of the house and across the patio. Being so small, it must have seemed like a three mile run.

Nonetheless, he did his business and turned shyly to look at me as I applauded his efforts. The look on his face with his bowed head was one of "Ooops!" as he realized he was at the edge of the grass and had missed it entirely.

He reached out again after the *three mile run*, running to

gleefully jump into my waiting hands as I assured him he had made a wonderful effort.

The man said he was pretty much trained outdoors, even though Puppers was only eight months old. The "accident" didn't matter to me because I had instantly felt a relationship was born that day.

He sniffed around the house. Dogs use their noses more than their eyes to see, you know. He played a bit with everything he could reach, which wasn't much, because when they called to tell me he was coming for a visit, I had hurried to *puppy-proof* the house per my friends' instructions.

The man handed me a partially chewed toy and a small baby blanket, then told me that Puppers got cold easily. He showed me how to put on the harness that Puppers would wear for a long time. I recall thinking, "He travels light, doesn't he?" But I was too excited to ask.

Four years later, and with a lot of sharing, caring and training for the **_both of us_**, I often wonder about all that had happened since that time. Again, that is why this book was born. But more importantly, the lessons of life fly in my face through my sometimes muddled brain and are now passed on to you.

As I held him in my arms that night, all I could think about were the words: **mutual compassion** . . . he cared about me and I cared about him. What a tiny, helpless little guy who lost his mom, dad, brothers and sisters. What a tragedy in just 8 short months…never to see any of them again…just as I had lost my family.

He came to me with only the proverbial "clothes on his back" and probably a good deal of emotional baggage.

But, wait a minute. He's waking up, wagging his tail, smiling in his own way and his paws are still rowing as he stands on his hind legs.

Despite all of his problem circumstances, he is still reaching out . . .

You know, God does that reaching out also if you think about it carefully. God doesn't carry around any baggage, no matter how light. ___So why should we?___ He sees it, forgives it and lets it go . . . moving on with His life, pursuing us in our lives, moving His hands toward us as He continues to say, "Come to Me. I want to hold you. I want a personal relationship with you. I want you to hold onto ME!"

That is what I meant by mutual compassion . . . God is a keeper of people. Once He gets hold of you, He won't let go.

Puppers taught me my first lesson when he arrived at my door. Puppers is a keeper also, and here he remains, through the good times and the rough times, the good memories and the heavy ones.

Dear Lord, keep me . . . and keep Puppers, too.

Lord, **YOU** still reach out . . . **PUPPERS** still reaches out . . . **I'M** still reaching out . . . help **others** to still reach out and may this book reach out to You with blessings.

Listen Up! Puppers Talkin' Here!

Hi! My name is Puppers. I snuck in here while Mama was asleep to use her 'puter to write this for you.

I come from a long line of Chihuahuas. They had me on a "farm" and my family was a mix of Chihuahua and pug. I had to laugh because my doctor now calls me a "Chipug" and Mama says there ain't no such name in the veterinarian book yet!

I guess they decided that I wasn't the type of dog they wanted, so they gives me to this big man named Moses. Honest! He was such a neat man, but he didn't have enough money to raise me. So he brought me here to Mama, even though I know Moses really wanted to keep me. I was just 8 months old when that happened!

At first, I felt like I was fallin' through the cracks of the "system," bein' shuffled about a lot in a short eight months. But Mama tells me God truly sent me to her. And I think He sent me, too.

The minute I saw her, I reached out my front paws to have her take me in her arms. Oh! She was so cuddly! I knew then that we would be a great match! Not many people who live together can say that they have a great match like we do!

Mama started to train me the first day. But I fooled her. I already knew what it meant to go outside for a few minutes several times a day! I fool her a lot when somethin' is not what I want to do, but don't tell her, okay?

When Mama got me, she had somethin' called *seizures* and they are from a brain tumor in her head. The first time she had one, I got really scared and all I could think to do was to crawl on her tummy while she lay on the carpet and kiss her as much as I could. It worked!

Mama talked to me a lot after that. She would play act havin' one of them seizures and I was s'posed to do two things. If she was standin' up, I was s'posed to tag her with my front paws on the front or back of her good leg so that she could sit down fast and not fall down. If she was holdin' me, then I kissed her left hand; her weak one; as fast as I could kiss it. Then she could hold onto the chair with her right hand and hopefully not slide out of it.

It took a LOT of work to help me learn to help her. We worked for four hours a day for about 5 weeks. But now I know how to do it without any problems at all. Mama says I know 34 diff'rent commands and things Mama is talkin' about with me. I don't know 'cause I can't count past four. She only taught me four single word commands. The rest of them are in phrases or sentences.

She tells me I am very smart; and I guess I am. It helps me to realize that no matter what, none of us is perfect. But we all have different talents we can use to help each other. I'll give you an example:

One of the neat things is that I also have seizures and Mama didn't know this when she got me. If anyone would have known, I think no one would have wanted to keep me. But Mama says it doesn't matter, 'cause it just means all the more that we are a perfect match for each other.

When I have my seizures, it's nice to wake up in Mamas' arms. She is cuddlin' me and singin' a Hebrew song to me or hummin' and talkin' to me softly.

I just wanted you to know that there are more important things than money, neat toys or even a perfect pet.

Those things are lovin', compassionin', carin', lettin' God handle the tough stuff and thankin' Him through the bad and good stuff. But most of all, the best is learnin' that even if you think no one ever loves you, God does and He is in charge of everythin'!!

I have the best of the best here . . . Mama does, too. And you know what is one of the most neatest things? We accept each other for who we are and we encourage each other...we have unconditional lovin' to give to each other and to others like you. It's just like the lovin' God gives to us.

You know what? If God can do that without lookin' at any of us as *diff'rent,* then why can't we? Maybe if you all read this book, it will help you to answer that question or help you to find out what is the bestest thing to do!

Oooops! Gotta go. Mama is wakin' up now and she promised me we'd go for a walk when she woke up.

I'll come back in to write more when I can 'cause, well, it IS her 'puter, but I really don't think she would mind, do you?

Your friend,

Puppers

MY Blankie

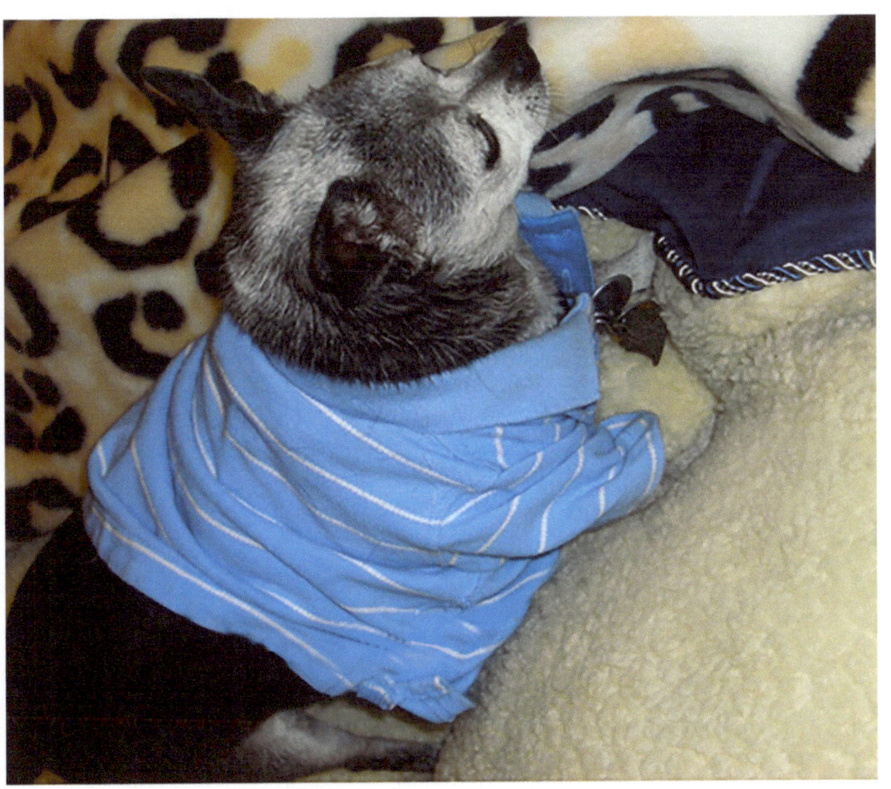

"Mama, it's MY blankie. I don't want ya to wash it!"

Grrrrrr! It's MY blankie.

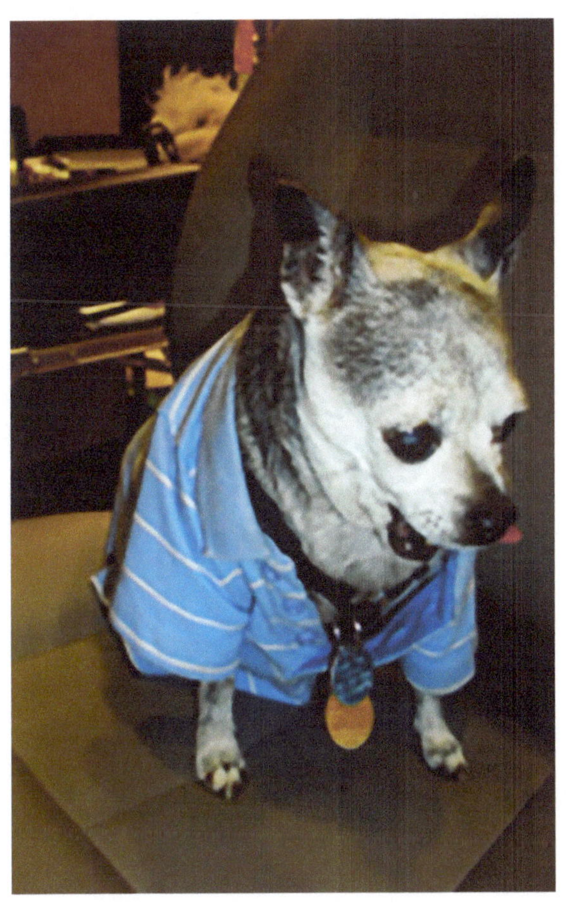

I said, "That's my blankie!!!!!!"

"Come on, Puppers. It's time to get up now."

"Aw, Mama, don' wanna get up!"

"You need to get up so I can wash your blankie, Puppers."

"Look, Mama, it ain't hardly dirty at all!"

"Pupppperrrssss . . .!"

"Okay, okay. But don't hurt it any, will ya?"

"No. I won't. In fact, you can sit here and watch it wash if you want to do that."

And he does . . . every once in a while for over an hour, he turns to look quickly at me, and then back to the washing machine.

I hung his blankie over the back of a chair to dry and part of it had to be on the seat. I left the room and he had jumped into the chair to lay on his blankie. I don't know if HE was giving the blankie comfort or if IT was easing HIS anxiety.

Life can be like a blankie, you know? We all have our things or people in life that we hang onto with all our might for security.

I don't want to call Jesus a *blankie*, but He is like that for a lot of people. The security He offers us goes far beyond any that a blankie can give, yet how many times a DAY do we carry HIS name around with us as we go through hardships, asking HIM for help and HIS ever-present love, comfort and guidance?

We don't literally hang onto a *blankie*. . . but we can hang onto Him tightly in these trying times.

For Puppers, there is security in seeing and touching; he's sort of like the *doubting Thomas* in this family . . . everything has to be orderly and scheduled for him. But with Jesus, we can rest assured that we reach Him instantly through the power of not only prayer, but just simply saying His NAME in the good AND the bad times.

If Puppers can reach out to a blankie for security, comfort and joy, just think how much and how often we can joyfully reach out to the One who will hold us when no one else will!!

For, you see, "blankies" don't hold us . . . Jesus does.

I Want It Yesterday!!

He taught me patience, the meaning of time . . . and about being impulsive. Impulsive means not being patient enough to wait and think about things first.

He sits, sometimes for an hour or more, waiting for me to shut down the computer. If I tell him to go in on the bed and lie down, he does it reluctantly, but sits there patiently also, waiting on me to be in the room with him.

He will sit with me and stare out the window for hours . . . . if we have time to do it . . . and all of this without a single whimpering complaint.

There is more to this thing about patience, time and being impulsive that I cannot quite see clearly . . . yet.

It seems that, if something is of the utmost importance to him, he is shouting in his quiet way, "I want it . . . yesterday!" But that isn't accurate either. It is simply a matter of HIM having HIS priorities straight. All of his ducks are in a row . . . and mine are not.

If I am upset with someone, I am apt to pick up the phone the minute I get home and call them to complain.

If I am sad, I'm apt to break into tears immediately.

Yes, there is something more to all of this that I can't quite figure out right now.

Maybe it is his example. He is always ready to please, follow directions, and to comfort me in times of distress. In fact, when I am stressed out, he seems to have a sixth sense that humans lack and he comes to me immediately . . . that must be the impulse.

It's an impulse that is positive, not only to comfort me but to just show me the positive sides of my life and then get me to move into *peace* inside me instead of *war*, *love* instead of *hate*, and to practice *patience* instead of being *impulsive*.

This has to be it. I don't have to demand, "I want it yesterday!' or be afraid and worried. With him, I can relax now and not have to stress out about his many tomorrows or mine.

God truly meant it when He said, "Cast your burdens on Me." He truly meant it when He said, "Don't worry about *anything*" and "My grace is sufficient for you."

You see, **God sent me His grace, which is something undeserved by me,** using a vessel to teach me patience, peace, love, joy and that there's a time for everything.

He sent me Puppers…and I am amazed that this little guy can teach me so much . . . and I DO have a lot to learn. The point is I'm learning . . . how about you?

THE LITTLE GUY

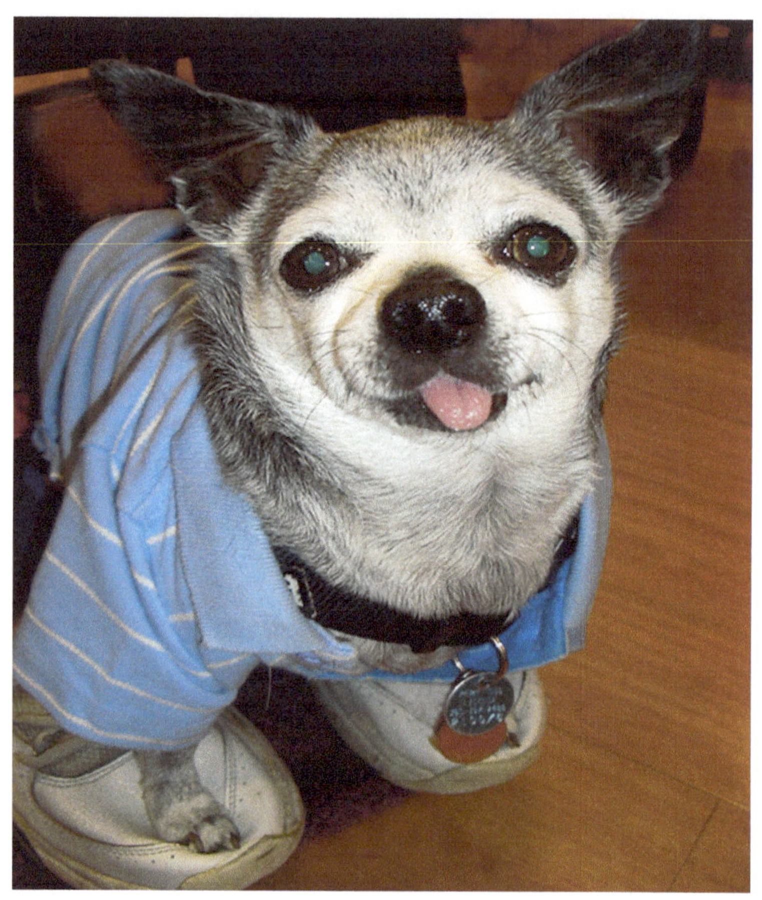

Hi! I almost fit into Mama's shoes

even though I'm a little guy!

"Mama, I don't like that lady!"

"Puppers, that isn't nice."

"But, Mama, I just don't like her!"

"Puppers, come here." He climbs up onto my lap. I hold him upright in my arms across my chest. And then he puts one paw on each side of my neck. When we have our talks, this is how he sits so we can look each other straight in the eyes.

"Puppers, we need to talk now, so listen very carefully, okay? Sometimes, especially now, there are things happening in this world that we don't like, so we need to begin to talk about those things because I believe you are old enough now to hear about them, find out what it all means and what you should do about it."

"But, Mama, I clearly see what happens. I'm a big boy now. My birthday is pretty soon. What am I gettin' for my birthday?"

"Well, Puppers, I know you're excited about that, so how about me giving you one of your presents now? It's the kind you can't play with and it isn't clothes or a snack, but it is something you can keep forever in your heart!"

"Forever, Mama? Really? I want that present right now!"

"Okay, then listen to this. Once upon a time, there was this little guy like you. He came to visit Mama. A man brought him and that little guy held his hands out, waving them at me like he was running in mid-air to get to me, so I took him out of the arms of the man and held him very close to my heart.

The man left and it didn't seem to bother the little guy. We got down on the floor and played a lot. Then he came over to me, got in my arms and fell asleep for quite a while. He was so little at that time that he drooled a little bit on my t-shirt.

Soon, the little guy woke up and I fixed us both some dinner. He made a mess with his food all over my nice clean floor."

"I betcha don't like that little guy anymore, huh, Mama?"

"No, Puppers. I cleaned up the mess and changed my shirt. Then the man called and asked if I wouldn't mind keeping the little guy overnight and he would come back to get him the next morning. I asked the little guy if that was okay with him . . ."

"Mama, you didn't reallllllllly keep him, did you????"

"Puppers, the little guy said he wanted to stay overnight just one time, so I said it was okay. He ran all over the house and got into EVERYTHING! Everything he could pick up, he tore up. I went around picking up the pieces. Those things he couldn't tear up, well, I put them up higher so he couldn't reach them."

"I betcha that made you hate him, didn'tja, Mama. Just like I hate that lady . . . I mean . . . I don't *like* that lady 'cause you told me we wasn't 'sposed to hate."

"Good boy, Puppers! You're right! We aren't supposed to hate anybody because Jesus never hated anybody."

"But, Mama, Jesus did! He got mad in that temple thingy and threw the peoples' stuff all over the place 'cause they messed up His Father's temple house!"

"Puppers, I don't want you to talk anymore right now. I just want you to listen to your present, okay?"

"Okay, Mama."

"Puppers, do you know what happened to that little guy?"

"Nooooooo . . ."

"Well, he stayed overnight. He slept beside Mama in bed and cuddled up to get warm. The next day, he was up bright and early, got off the bed and played all over the place, pulling at this and that until I had a terrible mess on my hands, just like Jesus did in the temple. I have to tell you, I was a little bit upset but I was more frustrated because I wasn't sure what I could do. Then the man called and asked if I wanted to keep the little guy forever."

"What?? I betcha you told him "no", didn'tja, Mama? I wouldn't have kept him. He was mean like that lady and I don't EVER want to see her anymore! I betcha kicked that little guy out quick, didn'tja!"

"No, Puppers. I didn't do that. I picked him up and gave him a present, just like the one I'm giving you today. I'm giving it to you right now. I'm giving you a big hug and kiss. I'm giving you the present of love. And, now I'm going to tickle you all over!!"

"Mama, I can't stop laughin'. Stop, Mama, stop!!! Ha, ha!! Stop!!"

"Puppers, now here is the best part of your present, so listen real close. Do you know who that little guy was?"

"No, Mama, but he ain't here, so you got rid of him, din'tja?"

"No, Puppers. I said to myself: I don't like some things this little guy has done since he came here, but I do like HIM! He is cuddly, loving, gives me a kiss once in a while, likes to play nice when he knows how to do that, stops doing something when I say he can't and seems to have a bit of love in him for other people. So I kept him . . . forever!"

"Wow, Mama! Where is he?"

"He's right here in my arms getting his birthday present, Puppers!"

"You mean, after he was not nice, you kept him anyway?!!"

"Yes, Puppers, I kept him anyway and I love him very much!"

"Wait. Wait a minute, Mama. I'm that little guy, ain't I?"

"Yes, Puppers, you are! Surprise!!"

"Mama, you mean you don't hate me for bein' a rotten little guy?"

"No, Puppers. I don't always like some of the things you do, but I don't hate YOU. I love YOU just like Jesus loved the people in the temple. He just didn't like the things they did, but He kept on loving them, no matter what . . ."

"So, I guess I gotta love that lady anyway, Mama, but can I still not like what she does sometimes?"

"That's your birthday present, Puppers. We learn to love people no matter what and we try to find something good about them, so you need to love this lady and find something you like about her."

"Wow! What a neat birthday present. So, I'm my own birthday present 'cause even though I wasn't a good little guy all the time, you still kept me and love me, Mama?"

"Yes, little guy . . . I'll keep you and love you forever . . . just like Jesus does."

"Mama, can we cuddle now, please??"

RADTELEVIDS

"Puppers! Time to come inside now! We need to get you ready for bed!"

There is so much on the information highway now, yet he still understands all of those words and goes straight into the bed. I believe he is a lot smarter than we give him credit for, however, we are all a lot smarter these days.

We sometimes get so much information that we get infected with what I call a **radtelevids** virus.

Remember when that didn't happen, even though we were all hungry for information of any sort? Remember when we used to all sit around the radio (**RAD**) to listen to stories, but also to get the news? Heaven forbid that anyone should change the channel if dad was listening to the news!

Then television (**TELE**) came on the scene and, even though there weren't many programs yet, people would sit around the TV as a family to watch what was then called decent programming. TV couldn't (and still doesn't) take the place of a nice family dinner at home with good conversation about the days' events, both personal and outside the home.

Now we deal with videos (**VIDS**). Unless we watch it with young children, most kids have their own electronical warehouse in their bedrooms. In fact, when punished for something they've done wrong, some kids are sent to their rooms where they spend the time either NOT thinking about what they did wrong or how they might correct it or learn from it. But instead, some will play around with their **electronicalwaregidgegadgets**.

I sit and play with words, just like that kid. However, I take time out for things of greater priority, like trying to remind people that God is in charge and needs all our attention to keep up a personal relationship with Him.

So, what has happened? Knowledge is a great thing, but too much radtelevids can do something horrible in personal relationships. Not only with others, but with our Father. The information can cause us to be overloaded where we "tune out", walking around listening to iPods or playing portable video games instead of looking at God's creation and other people. It can also get in the way of working towards more important things that we can and need to do. Like getting to know our Father in heaven, our family members, our friends and, yes, even new people we meet.

Next time we find radtelevid distractions happening, let's think of someone else and take time to get to know them. Take time to shut off the **radtelevids** and turn towards listening and talking with someone who may just simply need a kind word for the day.

I call Puppers into bed, even though there is a movie on TV that I reaaaaaaaaaaly want to see . . . but this is HIS time with me to relax, cuddle, play and feel very, very loved.

Love a lot today. Take the time. God wants to hear from you and so do others. God wants you to hear from HIM also.

May your RADTELEVIDS days be shorter and **_your relationships_** last longer!!

THE NO FEAR FACTOR

He's afraid of so many things. There's noises he doesn't recognize and doesn't remember. There are things that drop off counters near him and things that are bigger things than he is. He's shy around some people, but not afraid unless someone has treated him unkindly. He worries about when his dinner will be ready. He doesn't understand if we don't go out for the day, and I stay home to do things. There's so much for tiny Puppers to fear. Yet, I'm not sure he has experienced real terror. He might have felt it during the first time I had to leave him home alone. Right now, he is sleeping peacefully as I enter the door.

He then hears me call out, "Where's my gooood boy!!?" He shakes himself awake and comes flying off the bed where he was asleep on MY covers. It's something familiar to him, rather than his own blanket. But I don't mind. I just say a prayer of thanks that he is still okay, able to run and to cuddle with me. I've missed him as much as he's missed me.

No one seems to want to talk about terror these days. Are they immune to the chaos around us? Or do we hear so much about it that we feel overwhelmed? I define the term TERROR as simply, but devastatingly, a SEPARATION. It's a feeling of being totally alone in a crowd or alone altogether coupled with despairing helplessness.

It's not a joyful topic. But terror need not occur. I recall a married couple flying back to the West coast one time. They were being jostled around horribly by the winds hitting the jet. Yet they remained holding each other and talking calmly. Oh to be sure, there was probably some fear there, but not terror.

I had to ask myself, *Why aren't they feeling a state of terror*?

I know the answer to that. They were truly trusting Christian people. They **KNEW THEIR SAVIOR.** And no matter the outcome of what happens in this world, there would truly be **NO SEPARA-TION** for eternity between them and the only God who holds us in His loving, merciful arms.

We can listen to all the news accounts we want or have multiple tragedies in our lives. I've had my share in a short span of 6 years. I lost all of my immediate family members and two close friends. And so has Puppers. But we have to **CHOOSE** whether to feel the terror of SEPARATION or to feel the contented comfort of ___BELONGINGNESS___ with our Savior. Belongingness stops fear cold.

I've said it before to others….Puppers knows who his **CREATOR** is, so I don't think he can experience true terror as we humans do. Maybe this is one of the best things Puppers, in his own small world, can teach us: "God is with us ALWAYS, even unto the end . . ."

I choose **ETERNAL BELONGINGNESS** with no fear . . . and I believe Puppers does, also.

'Lectrical Stuff and Gidgegadgets

Wow! Today was really a tough one, even though I had a nice day yesterday taking a long walk with Mama. It was so sunny and warm. But, today was different. I woke up and was crawling on the floor. Mama said, "Good morning, Scooter!" I wagged my tail at her.

I no more than gets near her when real quick like, there was a sound I heard that Mama didn't seem to hear. With a big flash of light, I ran into her arms realllly fast . . Boom!

Then there was another flash and another boom. I looked out the windows and there was hard white stuff hittin' the roof that I could hear and then it was hittin' the ground. It was the size of small peas. Mama said, "It's okay, Puppers. It is just like boom-booms. Do you remember when we had boom-booms on the Fourth of July? Well, this is like boom-booms then and it is okay."

"Hey, what is that white stuff, Mama?"

"It's called *hail*, Puppers, and it won't last long."

"Promise?"

"Yes, I promise, Puppers."

Well, she was right, but that boom-boomin' and lights flashin' lasted longer. Finally, it quit and there was just a lot of rain.

I went outside later and I couldn't keep myself from lookin' up at the sky.

Mama told me it would be okay to watch the sky, but not to be afraid because someday Jesus would come back ridin' on one of those nice fluffy clouds and then we would go home to be with Him.

I asked her if He would have boom-booms and lights when He came and she grinned. "Yes, Puppers, but it will be nice sounding boom-booms and very pretty lights."

I came back inside then and Mama was workin' on the 'puter. She plugged somethin' in the back that her auntie had give her. It was somethin' called 'speakers'.

"Mama, I thought *we* was speakers."

"We are, Puppers, but we're a different type of speakers. We're *people speakers* and so we talk about things like Jesus. These speakers play nice music." Then she turned it on.

BOOM!!! Louder boom-booms!!! I ran to my hidey-hole under the bed. She was working on the buttons to try and get it turned down, I guess.

She called me and told me it was okay now. I came into the livin' room, but I sure didn't wanna do that! She picked me up and I could hear soft music, but when it quit, there was a buzzin' sound each time she touched another button. I kept tryin' to tell her it wasn't safe! I could almost picture it burnin' her 'puter.

Finally she turned it all off and agreed with me. She took that wire out.

Now, all I gots to say is that I don't think I like *'lectrical stuff* and *gidgegadgets,* but I guess we have to learn to be careful with them just like we learns to be careful to tell others about Jesus and what we says to them.

Boom-booms, gidgegadgets and 'lectrical stuff is things I don't wanna fool around with 'cause they can be dangerous if you don't knows what you is doin', but Jesus will do those things and HE knows what HE'S doin', so that's okay by me.

Think I'll just follow Him….how 'bout you?

TAG, MAMA! YOU'RE IT!

Puppers is 'sleeping in' this morning, so I told him I would write his story this time. He wanted me to write about the game of *tag*.

Some people play different games of tag. Some are fun and some are not so fun. Play Puppers version and you have a fun game of tag.

I usually get up around eight in the morning. And when I hear Puppers sneeze or sniffle, I know he is awake and ready to get up.

Most mornings, I see him before he gets close to me. Then it is like I have spoiled his game. This morning, for example, I didn't see him. All I felt was his front paws touching my slipper and he was off and running for the door yelling, "Tag, Mama! You're it!"

I took off after him, but I have a disadvantage . . . I'm the one who has to open the door. He takes this in good humor, waiting for me to pet him, open the door, pat his back and say, "Now, Puppers. Tag! You're it!" He runs to the backyard and I yell, "Oh, what a happy puppy!", as he stands there wagging his tail.

Now, in the game of tag, he really is supposed to run back and tag me. But he hasn't learned that yet, just like we all need to learn how to play a game or **do other things in life**. He just sits on the grass and grins back at me. This seems like such a silly thing to write about, giving human traits to an animals. But it really is important to let others know why I sometimes do it. Some people get the reality of **BODY LANGUAGE . . . the only way Puppers has to communicate with me . . . the realization that this is the *good tag* game.**

Other people just don't get it . . . that is the not-so-fun game of tag. You have to work harder at trying to find out what they want or what their needs are. Sometimes, we just have to simply go away and leave them alone until they are ready to communicate.

I'm thinking about someone most of us care a lot about who said, "Body language has absolutely NOTHING to do with EFFECTIVE communication."

That person isn't getting along well with others. That person doesn't realize that their own body language speaks VOLUMES about their personality and I think they expend a lot of energy trying to hide their body language.

You all know that Puppers and I have long conversations. I sort of have to *read his mind*; the body language tag game; and that can be very hard to do. But it is well worth the effort so that I can meet his needs and he can meet mine.

It is sort of like body language tag with Puppers and I. It is the fun kind. **It is the meaningful and fulfilling kind, whether it is negative or positive body language. Because the point is this, AT LEAST WE ARE STILL COMMUNICATING.**

With the person we all care about, it is less meaningful and fulfilling because of that person's **disbelief in body language as an effective communication tool and because of the MIXED MESSAGES** of out-of-control, and possibly unrealized, body language sent to us and others.

For example, Puppers could just simply walk around and ignore me, then suddenly jump into my arms and kiss me a lot. I would receive a mixed message of whether he wants me around or not.

It is the same with humans. We can send out **honest** body

language that matches our words, thoughts and feelings, or we can send out mixed messages . . . sort of like slapping someone when one is smiling the whole time.

Whatever the case, let's not be fooled. Body language is VERY important to communication. If used effectively, it becomes a fun game of tag between Puppers and I, but when used successfully between human beings, it is powerful and gives us all Christ-like people skills that exhibit the fruits of the Spirit from me to you and you to me.

"Come on, Puppers. Let's go play a game of fun tag!" He wags his tail, and then he is off and running. His body language corresponds with his feelings and we have effectively communicated.

How is YOUR game of tag today? "Ours is great, huh, Puppers?"

Hospitals, Uncle Doctors and *Strongness*

"I'm a good rassler, ain't I?!!!"

I'm sitting in the 'hospital.' I'm actually on my bed trying to sew an arm back on a stuffed bear that Puppers had been wrestling with, He calls it *rasslin'* and the bear is one of Puppers' favorite toys.

"Watcha doin', Mama?"

"Well, Puppers, Bear has a boo-boo and Mama is going to try to fix it for him."

"What? How did he get that boo-boo?" Puppers is watching so carefully. It's as if he is not only worried that I will find out how Bear got this boo-boo, but also showing compassion in his eyes about his poor friend.

"He has to get some stitches in his arm, Puppers, so his arm won't hurt anymore."

"Oh, I 'member. I did that the other day. I was playin' with him and he gots a little rough when we was rasslin', so his arm sort of was fallin' off. I'm sorry, Bear!"

Puppers reaches up to kiss him. He has been sitting on the bed with his eyes wide open watching every stitch I put in the stuffed bears' arm to reattach it.

"Be careful, Mama! Is he cryin' like I did when I had to go see uncle Dr. Roy to get a shot?"

"No, Puppers. He's not crying. But you know, some of us do cry and we cry a lot."

"I did the other day when you was gone to the doctors' office 'cause I missed you!"

"Well, Puppers, what did I tell you that you need to do when you feel like crying or when you see someone else cry?"

"Oh, I know! I know! I'm 'sposed to pray to Jesus and that will help us feel better!"

"That's right!"

"We sure pray a lot to Him, don't we, Mama? Is that 'cause you said Jesus can fix anything?"

"Yes, Puppers, He can!"

"Well, when bear got his arm hurt, how come we don't take him to see uncle Dr. Roy or uncle Dr. Jim? Uncle Dr. Roy could fix him like uncle Dr. Jim fixes you."

"Puppers, Jesus uses a lot of people to help us get all fixed up. He shows us the right people to go to for help.

You get your medicine and your shots from uncle Dr. Roy and uncle Dr. Jim helps Mama. I guess Jesus just felt like I could be the one to help bear this time."

"Jesus is pretty smart, huh, Mama?"

"Yes, He is, Puppers."

"Mama, sometimes some things don't get fixed. How come, Mama?"

"Well, Puppers, it just means we have to pray more to Jesus and wait on Him to answer because He has things all worked out so that something or someone comes along to help us. Just like now. You're really nervous having to wait to see if we can fix Bear, aren't you? Remember when my head was hurting? Uncle Dr. Jim sent me to a different doctor who could help me. Then you came along to live with me and help me when I was going to have a seizure. That was TWO good things that happened from one tiny little prayer and waiting for Jesus to answer it!"

I hand him Bear. "He's good as new, Puppers."

"Mama, some people pray and some people don't. I thinks they would get a really big surprise just how much Jesus will do. Lookit! Bear wants to play now! This pray thing really works!"

"Yes, Puppers, when we pray, we all get stronger, because Jesus gives us HIS strongness to help us!"

"Well, Mama, I better pray a little more now, 'cause Bear is stronger and I think he's gonna win this rasslin' match this time. If I get hurt playin', Mama, you gots to 'member to pray first and then call uncle Dr. Roy, okay?"

"Okay, Puppers, you can count on Jesus and on me."

WHAT'S WRONG WITH THIS PICTURE?

"Mama, who's that kid?

"Hey! Come back here! Leave that alone! Hey, you, come here! Stop that!" (pant, pant) "Stop running so fast! Aha! Gotcha!"

Puppers has the new kid laying on his back with his paws on the new kids' belly as if he has won a major wrestling match.

"Puppers, come here a minute."

"But, Mama, he was runnin' all over the place. I mean, I had to stop him, Mama. He was tryin' to take all my toys! Mama, I was . . . I mean, honest, Mama, that new kid just don't know what to do!"

"It's okay, Puppers. Listen now. This new kid doesn't know what to do. He's just a little guy. He's like your babies in the nursery. He's only eight weeks old!"

"Wait a minute, Mama!!! There he goes again!" (pant, pant) "Gotcha! Mama, I gots to hold him right here! What's he doin' here, anyway, Mama??"

"Puppers, he's the new kid that lives up the block and we're watching him for his Mama while she gets a drink of water. We're just going to watch him for a little while. Why don't you try to share your toys with him? Maybe, if you try and talk to him nicely, he'll be nice."

"Okay, Mama, I'll try, but if he doesn't do what I tell him to do, I'll have to rassle him down again!"

The race is on. Puppers is chasing the new kid. Puppers is right. That new kid is just not listening.

(pant, pant) "Mama! Mamaaaaaaaaaaa! He just don't stop. What's wrong with him, Mama?"

"Puppers, do you remember when you were a little baby?"

"Sort of, Mama."

"Well, Puppers, you were doing the same things this new kid is doing."

"Ah, Mama, I wasn't that bad!"

"Puppers, I'm afraid you were doing the same things and some of them were just as wrong to do."

"But, Mama, you never told me I was a bad boy."

"That's right, Puppers, because I never wanted you to feel that you were bad. You just didn't know the right things to do.

"Remember when I showed you how I learned to do coloring? I had some trouble staying inside the lines and then I *practiced* quite a lot until I could do it the right way to make it look pretty. Nobody told me I was bad. I needed to learn how to color because, later in life, I wanted to be able to use the computer to draw pictures and make them look nice." Puppers turns his head sideways.

"Puppers, when you look at the new kid, look at him like a picture in a coloring book. Tell me what you think is wrong with that picture."

"Well, Mama, first of all, he just plain don't listen to nobody!"

"That's true, Puppers. I didn't listen either for a while and neither did you. What else do you see, Puppers?"

"Well, I guess he might need a little help. He is kinda cute. You know, Mama, just like somebody showed you how to color better, maybe there isn't really anything wrong with the picture. Do you think maybe it's because he's just *new*?"

"Puppers, I think you have found the answer. He is **different . . . and** nice.

"What's *diff'rent* mean, Mama?"

"Do you look like me in the mirror, Puppers?"

"Noooo."

"We don't look the same or always act the same. That's what makes us different. We're different in how we walk, talk, think, and feel on the inside AND we're different looking on the outside."

"So, if he is *diff'rent*, Mama, what does I *do* with him?"

"Puppers, what do you think Jesus would say?"

"Well, in that big book you read; the Bible; Jesus was around all sorts of diff'rent people . . . lame, blind, nice, not so nice . . . hmmmmmmmmmm . . . maybe what's wrong with this picture is that I'm not bein' nice to someone who is diff'rent than me?"

"Puppers, I think you just figured it out. Maybe it doesn't matter that he is different. You need to stay the same nice boy you are and maybe you can help him by being his friend!"

"Hmmmm . . . okay. Hey, buddy, want to come play with my 'raffe' (giraffe)? Come on. I'll show you how to play with him so he don't get hurt 'cause he's a lot littler than we are, but he sure is nice!"

he don't get hurt 'cause he's a lot littler than we are, but he sure is nice!"

GOD, ME, PUPPERS, ROOTINE AND NICE . . .

"Mama, people says I'm spoiled. Does that mean my expiration date has come around?"

"Puppers! Where did you learn those big words?!"

"I been peekin' at your dishionary!"

"Oh, you mean my *dictionary*."

"Yeah, but Mama, is I spoiled?"

"Well, Puppers, yes, I guess you are a little spoiled. I think there are ELEVEN Commandments. You don't lie to people or little kids. The 11th one is, "Thou shalt not lie to man's best friend." You see, Puppers, when people tease you and say you are spoiled, it means that you get some special treatment. Like when I take an extra T-shirt for you or when I wrap you in your blankie and put you inside my coat to keep you warm. Most puppies don't get so cold and they don't mind the cold weather."

"Oh. Then I'm not spoiled, Mama, I'm just happier! Ha! Ha!"

"Yes, Puppers, that must be it. See, you have your own routine sometimes!

"What's a *rootine*, Mama?"

"Well, it means you do things a certain way. You do them like you want to do them and when you want to do them. Let's talk about your routine. You sleep on the bed under your covers with Mama at night. You get up in the morning when you are ready. You go outside and when you have done your running around, you take a long slow walk around the entire fence to check things out.

"You do that because I have told you that is your job. Then you come back inside, race for your food dish, find it is empty, and that it's not time for breakfast yet. Then you run really fast to sit in front of the heater to get warm.

"I have my coffee and look at my emails. That is when you are really polite and let me do those things. Then you come in to barely peek around the corner at me to see if I'm finished. If I'm not, you back away and go to the heater again or lie on the bed.

"When you hear my chair squeak, you come running. I'm making another cup of coffee. You listen for the *ding-ding* on the microwave cooker. You peek around the corner of the cabinet at me. I ask if you are hungry and you wag your tail wildly. Then I fix your breakfast and mine.

"YOU always wait until I am finished with my breakfast because you hope I will give you some of mine. Then you eat yours. Next, you sprawl out on the rug in front of the heater. Now do you know what *routine* means?"

"Yeah, it means that I'M the one who gets to pick what I wants to do for the day, huh, Mama?"

"Let's put it this way, Puppers. God lets me pick what I want to do for the day, but HE directs me as to which way to go about doing it. I pick what you are to do for the day (shhh . . . don't tell Puppers, but some of it is what I pick out and the rest is just plain stubborn on HIS part) and then you do that. Or, sometimes you find a better way to do it. Or, sometimes you sort of do what you want anyway.

It doesn't matter. God lets you pick out what you want to do and then He helps even YOU to do it the way **_HE_** wants."

"Whaaaat??? You mean God is the boss over you AND me?? You mean He has me doin' what HE wants and it just seems like I'm doin' what I want?"

"Yes, Puppers, that's about the size of it. God is in charge of everything you do and everyone, including you!"

"Wow! Is that why you is always tellin' me not to worry, but to let God take care of it?"

"Yup…you got it!"

"Then, Mama, is God spoilin' me or you?"

"Puppers, I think God is spoiling both of us with His blessings!"

"Then, Mama, I don't think I is spoiled. And all of that ain't *rootine*. I'd call it . . . reaaaaaly nice!"

(From: Proverbs 16:9 . . A man's heart plans his way, but the Lord directs his steps).

Loop-de-loop

I am still trying to figure out all these things you have learned, 'cause you are older than me.

For instance, there is a place near where we live that Mama takes me for a walk. I call it the *loop-de-loop,* 'cause it just goes 'round and 'round in a biiiiiig circle. It is really neat. though. I gets to see chickens and roosters; cock-a-doodle-dooooo! And there's so many squirrels that I can't count them yet 'cause I'm only in the *first grade* now. But I do get to chase them squirrels. I never get to catch 'em, though, 'cause they run faster than me.

Hmmmm . . . maybe that's 'cause when I go for my walk I have to wear a harness and a leash. Do you think being tied down like that is the reason the squirrels is faster than me?

I noticed this thing of being tied down with a lot of people, too. But it is really weird 'cause I can't **SEE** their harness or leash. Wonder what holds them back?

I hear 'em talkin' 'bout it all the time. Even the little kids. They say it's 'cause they are too busy. Too busy to stop and sniff the flowers or call out to someone or even just to say *Hello* to someone they meet! Lots of these people I meet say *Hello* to me and tell me how cute I am. Maybe if I tried to stay cuter, they will take time to relax for a few minutes and they might not feel so tied down, at least for a little while.

See, we went shoppin' the other day and Mama took me in the store scooter for the first time. I got a little scared 'cause she tied my leash to the basket we was ridin' in. She said it was so I wouldn't fall out. So maybe it is good to be tied down sometimes.

Anyway, I had fun in that scooter . . . zoom, zoom, zooooom!

People we went by tried to stop and pet me. Mama would slow the scooter down and let them do it, but then she said somethin' 'bout *time* and "We have to hurry now or we'll miss our big bus to take us home." Maybe this thing called *time* is what ties us all down, do ya 'spose? I mean, I would really be afraid if we missed the big bus to get home. 'Cause that would mean a lot of walkin' to do and I'm just a little guy! So maybe being afraid ties us down, too.

I asked Mama about all this when we was gettin' on the big bus and she agreed I could be right. She said that fear and time might tie us *all* down from liking life a lot. Well, for now, I like life a lot, 'cept for the times I'm tied down.

See, there is a time to be tied down, like when I'm in the scooter so I can be safe. And there is a time *not* to be tied down. Like when you want to stop and smile at people. Yes, puppies DO smile, and just take time to say *Hello*!

Mama says that Jesus didn't let things or people tie Him down. He always made time to stop and help them . . . or say *Hello,* or hold them like when He held the little kids. And He also made time to pray. I guess He didn't think time or fear of no time was as important to Him as it is to us. I mean, time is important to me and the fear of losing time is important, especially like when it's time to eat or time to go bye-bye.

Must be that some things is more important to do in our lives then other things, hmmmm?

If you ask me, being tied down is sometimes not a good thing, 'cause we only look at ourselves then. And Mama says that Jesus didn't want us to do that.

He wants us to share life with others, help them, be nice and most of all, share our lives with Him.

So getting tied down with a lot of junk in our lives isn't such a good thing after all, hmmm? Well, I think when Mama says prayers tonight, I'm gonna pray for Jesus to help me understand this *tied down* thing a little better.

I know one thing about it though: if I ever have to be tied down, I can't think of a nicer person to be tied down with and that person is Jesus. I don't want to be tied down by unhealthy fear and lack of time. I'd rather be tied down with Jesus and the way He handled this 'tied down' thing.

How 'bout you?

Well, I may be tied down now, but look out squirrels!!!! Here comes Puppers!!!!!!!

Invisible Winds

It's interesting to watch Puppers in the yard, especially during the time of autumn. He gets very engrossed in the leaves that swirl around and I tease him when he chases them. Is he part cat or what?

The hardest part for him is that he cannot see the wind. He just feels it, looks at the sky clouds for long periods of time, and watches the leaves blowing in the trees. He starts barking if it is really windy and begins to run around the yard as if he is upset because he can't catch the wind. He can't see it, so he can't attack it and get it to stop blowing.

Not being able to see the wind must be confusing to him, as it would be to us. At times, we get broadsided by the winds of life. We can't see it. We can only feel it. And we can't stop it . . . The winds of life just happen.

It reminds me of the story about Peter that I read to Puppers recently. The men were out in a boat way past dark, which made things even worse. The wind picked up and they were getting broadsided by it. They were very afraid. But then a new *wind* blew in across the waters and they became terrified. They thought they were seeing a ghost . . . this new type of wind.

However, Peter, who was always ready to jump right in and fight or at the very least, test the situation, said, "Lord, if that is You, bid me come to You on the water!"

Now, big winds can be very loud. I can envision him leaning way out over the boat with his hands cupped over his mouth and shouting. All the Lord said was one simple word, "Come." And Peter did.

He had so much faith in the Lord at the moment that it incredibly took over his fear. This *wind* sound, when it said, "Come", was inspiring much more confidence in him than the other wind. I think that is why Peter stepped out of the boat. He had confidence in THIS new *wind* alone.

Now, don't be upset with me for comparing Jesus to the wind . . . It is just a mere, but strong analogy.

Suddenly, Peter is looking at Jesus and walking on the water. I often wonder what was going through his mind. I have a feeling he was so in awe of Jesus that his mind went blank. Which, to me IS THE PRECISE TIME WHEN FAITH CAN ENTER IN.

We seem to feel Jesus being in our lives during the blank and broken times we might have happening.

But then, Peter broke his thought pattern of "Jesus only" and focused on the other wind, the one that was broadsiding all of them. The one that I call the winds of life . . . the wind that could be the death of him . . . wind that is called the "I" in all of us . . . ***pride.*** "Hey, look at ME! I can walk on water!" It was somewhat like the eye (I) of a hurricane, but different.

If he kept focused ***only on Jesus,*** that eye (I) of the hurricane would be calm. It would calm the winds of this life and all the worries he (and we) pack around.

But no, Peter had to focus INSIDE SELF… and that is when he began to sin. That is when the OLD SELF WIND broadsided him. That is when he knew he needed Jesus more than ever. That is when his "I" in pride began to swallow him up.

That is when, most definitely, HE made the choice to go with

<u>the winds of Jesus' life . . . TRUE life . . . found only in Christ.</u>

Something stronger than the winds of life will take over in Peter, and in us. It is pure faith . . . indescribable faith, that will make us call out for Jesus. And this is the best part . . . the WIND will catch US!

May your faith

let the wind

catch you today . . . it's worth it!

CARE TO SHARE

Since both you and I know that puppies can't talk, I had to sneak in here to write this while Mama takes a nap . . . shhh. We need to be very quiet.

When I first came to live here, I found out that Mama was a teacher and she told me then that I was like a pre-schooler. Then I graduated to kindergarten. After I learned some more stuff, she let me graduate to first grade on my birthday, but the best part is that she bought me a new puppy of my own. He is white with red ears! I can throw him high in the air. And most of the time, we play with him at night on the bed. We play rasslin' matches. I wins all the time 'cause I'm a good rassler!

Anyway, if puppies could REALLY talk, then boy, do I have a lot to tell you!

Mama started right away showing me what to do around here. I have a really nice place to live in and a big backyard to play in.

I go out to the backyard to bark at the birds and I let the squirrels run on top of the fence. But boy, if they gets in my backyard, I really kick up a fuss. It's MY backyard!

One thing Mama is teaching me, though, is to SHARE. That was part of the test to go into first grade.

I see the neighbors here and they don't share. They fight all the time or steal from each other. We have one neighbor that we like, though, and her name is Aunt Lani. She has an older dog named Jakers. Jakers and I get to play in my backyard, like today, when the weather is nice.

I kind of have to watch Jakers, though, 'cause he is an old boy and he can't play as rough as I do. We are good friends. I've even showed him where my room is and where I sleep. I showed him where all my toys are and let him play with some of them. I showed him where he could get a drink of water.

Now, I usually eat all of my food, but today, I saved some for Jakers and he really liked it. He told me Mama serves up pretty good chow and he ate the rest of my chicken and rice. Mama told me I was a good boy to share with him.

Then Jakers and I got something really nice! We got a treat! I saw Mama give Jakers an extra piece, but that was okay. She told me he was our *guest,* so when we got to aunt Lani's I got a little extra . . . You see, it all evens out in the end!

Why is it that some people can't relax like us puppies and see that! I learned that part about a lot of people; this **not** sharing thing. I thought it was one of the rules that Jesus told us about, but I guess people don't believe it is really something we need to do. I mean, if I am a puppy and can share with others why can't others do the same thing? It gets really confusing at times.

There are a lot of rules to learn. I think I have done really well with this.

You know, I think learning **WHO** the rules came from and that they are there so we can show others the LOVE of Jesus by sharing, is the important thing to remember and that is what helps us to keep those rules.

When Mama and I read the Bible together, we learnt that Jesus died on the cross for us. But before He did that He shared two big rules with us: to love God and to love one another.

When you think about it, love is sharing everything you have because you care about the other person, like I care about Jakers. It's just as much as Jesus cared for you. He cared soooo much that He died on the cross for us. He shared His life TOTALLY and the least we can do is to love God, love Jesus, and show that love by loving our neighbors, even Jakers.

Well, I see Jakers wants to play some more. Sometimes we have to remind each other to share. But that is one of the best parts 'bout bein' friends and lovin' each other.

I hope you try to have many of those 'sharin'' days, too!

"It's MY Cadillac convertible, Mama!!"

MY CADILLAC CONVERTIBLE

"Puppers, where are you? Puppers, come now please!"

Well, I can't find him right now. I guess I'll wash my hands and face. Maybe then Puppers will come. He's probably laying under the bed right now in his hidey-hole.

"Oh my gosh!"

"Puppers! Are you okay? What are you doing under there?"

"Mama, I was just sleepin."

"Ahhhh! Come here, Puppers. I want to talk to you. Were you having a good dream?

"Yeah, Mama. I was dreamin' 'bout the new scooter. Mama, is this thing yours or mine?"

"Well, Puppers, I think it belongs to both of us, don't you?"

"But, Mama, I don't think that you drive it too well. 'Member the other day when you crashed it into the wall?

"Well, I'm not sure you can drive it very good, Mama. I mean, well I mean, well, I don't know what I mean. I'm sorry, Mama, I didn't mean to hurt your feelings. It's just that I get kinda scared, you know? Why don't you let me try to drive it, Mama?"

"Well, Puppers, I don't think that people would let you drive such a big scooter. By the way, it's okay if you tell me in a nice way that I don't drive very well now. Mama used to drive a car a long time ago and I'm not used to doing that anymore, even with the little thing like a scooter.

"Remember each time we come into the house, as we come in the door, you tell me, "Turn it, Mama!" And then you tell me when to turn it into the other room. That is sort of like driving it, isn't it?"

"Yes, Mama, I guess I am helping you to drive it, aren't I?"

"Yes, Puppers. Remember when we talked about 'sharing' things? Well, we share almost everything in the house.

"We share some of our food. We share the bed. We share the television set. We share the backyard.

"But, it would be hard, Puppers, if I were to try to wear your T-shirt, wouldn't it? And what if you tried to wear my clothes, Puppers?"

"HAAA! That's funny, Mama! I wouldn't be able to wear your clothes, Mama. They're too big!!"

"Yes, Puppers, that would look kind of funny, wouldn't it?

"Puppers, you never did tell me about your dream. Do you want to tell me about it now?"

"Oh, Mama! Boy, it was a neat dream! I dreamed I was ridin' on the scooter. I was on the chair, and not on the runnin' board. It didn't matter that it doesn't have a gas pedal. I could steer with the handlebars and get it to go by pressing on that throttle thingy on the handlebars you use. Then, all of a sudden, this old scooter turned into the most beautiful yellow Cadillac convertible!

"I was ridin' down the freeway and I heard you yellin' at me. You yelled, "Puppers, come back!" Then I got really scared, Mama, because I didn't know how to back up __MY__ yellow Cadillac convertible."

"Puppers, that sounded like a neat dream, but a very scary one. Do you think that maybe this is why we are supposed to share things?"

"Mama, do you mean if we share things like Jesus wants us to do, then maybe we can help each other out when we get into trouble?"

"Yes, Puppers, I think Jesus wants us to share anything we have so that we can learn to love each other and help each other. Think about it. If we share things, we can even have twice the fun. Just like right now. How about you and I get on the scooter and go for a ride? While we are riding, we can share the fun of thinking that we are riding in a Cadillac convertible!"

"Mama, can it still be a yellow color?"

"Puppers, I think we can talk about that and share any color we want our Cadillac convertible to be."

"Let's go, Mama! I want to see what it looks like with red and blue checkered squares on it. HA! HA!"

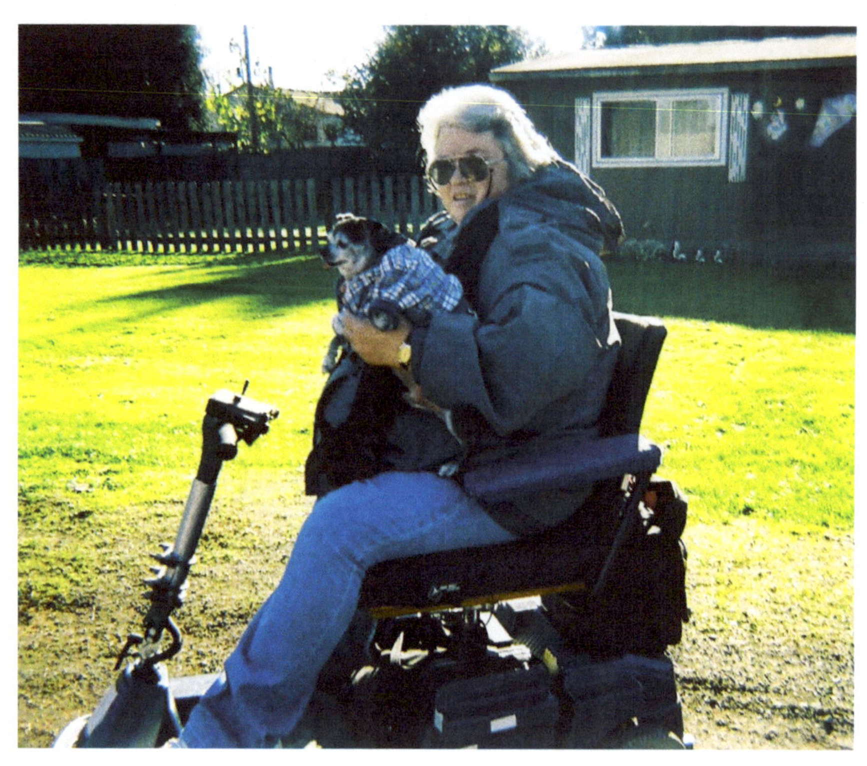

OUR Cadillac convertible

HE'S HERE WITH YOU

"Mama! Mama, I don't feel so good . . ."

At that point, I didn't even get to answer Puppers. All I could do was watch him as he tried to crawl to me and I ran to pick him up.

He had been lying on the bed. We had had a wonderful day. He'd been able to go to the library with me and run on the grass, smelling all the new smells. He was petted by lots of people in the library and then had lunch at the nearby park while we watched the "big birdies" take off and land. That's his name for jets.

Then we came home to rest. And when he woke up we went for another ride. After that, he got to play with his friend, Oscar, a new dachshund living with my friend next door.

I brought him home and we ate dinner together . . . but . . . shortly after that, Puppers had a very long seizure. I put him gently in the middle of the bed as I searched frantically through my back-pack to find his injectable medication.

I gave that to him and prayed. I just kept saying, "Lord, hold him. Help him."

He seemed to be coming out of it, so I sat him on the bed. But he had difficulty standing up. His legs and whole body can be very weak after a seizure like that. I picked him up again and he began to jerk . . . going into another long seizure. I gave him more medication.

I continued praying and began to cry. Finally, he snapped out of it and awoke in my arms, kissing me and not wanting me to put him down.

I held him for what seemed an eternity and thanked God that he was okay.

It may seem strange to care so much for an animal like I do for Puppers. But he is family to me. Just as much as my aunt, uncle and cousins.

More importantly, God gave him to me through a friends' kind donation . . . But God gave me more than that when Puppers arrived.

I have seizures and had always been afraid; more like TERRI-FIED; when friends told me what happened during MY seizures.

God sent Puppers. Puppers has seizures, too. I'M LESS AFRAID OF MY OWN SEIZURES BECAUSE I'VE NOW SEEN WHAT IT IS LIKE WHEN PUPPERS HAS A SEIZURE.

I try to relax now and it works. I still have seizures and so does Puppers. Both of us know one thing, HE'S HERE WITH US!

Not too many people are fortunate to even realize that He's always there. He will hold us, lead us, guide us and love us with an unconditional love and compassion that maybe, just maybe, we need to learn to share with others.

He's always there . . . I know it. And Puppers knows it.

I beg you, before it is too late, to always know that

HE'S HERE WITH US

for you . . . for everyone.

YARD BRUSHES

"Mama! Come quick! That guy is here to give my lawn a haircut!!!!"

This summer, Puppers has stayed outside like clockwork on Thursday mornings, waiting for this event. Our grass has some dry patches that look like straw. After the grass gets mowed, he loves to go to those patches, lie down on the ground on his back and get it "scritched." It must be a wonderful feeling for him to be scratched like that.

This reminds me of dry patches in our *lives*. You know, when things are going along just okay or *so-so*. We get comfortable during those times. At least I know I do. We seem to take things for granted.

I would be the least of people to tell you all about the wrong things in this world, all the worries and all the frustrations that people go through, Christian or non-Christian. I can remember back when I was a non-Christian and those things would make me cringe. I just kept plowing on through like a lawnmower, certain if I could just get a *lucky break*, then things would be okay.

I then became a Christian and of course, realized that life is not a series of *luck*. But life is a series of blessings and miracles, hills **and** valleys that we all go through. That old familiar saying of "Christians aren't born to be comfortable" really rings true in the valleys.

I'm in a deep valley again now. I'm struggling with a lot of pain. And yet, I can no longer take it for granted that it is "just one of those things."

I have to take a deeper look at it. But at the same time, I'm more accepting of it. I'm surely NOT loving it. I realize that there is a time for change, a time for pain, a time for a lot of other things and a time to continue to let God take control. As I grow older, there will be more pain or less of it.

The point is this: I can still do the small things, like watching Puppers roll around in the grass and enjoy his "scritching." I can still realize with all my heart that God is by my side with the Holy Spirit watching and comforting my soul. I can realize that the promises of God are true as I rest, read my Bible more and get into a closer relationship with God.

I cannot get into a close relationship with *luck*, but I can do that with God.

Dry patches have a GOOD purpose in our lives and Puppers has reminded me of that every day this summer, just as if God were saying, "Look at him. He doesn't expect ALL the grass to be green. He even loves the dry patches."

May the "yard brushes" of your life do the same for you with God leading you.

Friend or Fiend

"Puppers, come inside right now!" He walks in with his head hanging low.

"What, Mama?"

"Did I just hear you calling someone a name outside?"

"Yes, Mama, but they called **ME** one **FIRST!**"

"Does that make it okay for you to call them a name?"

"Well, it made me feel better!"

"Awe, Puppers, we talked about this before. And I guess you still don't understand it yet."

"I unnerstand that it makes me mad when they call me a name!"

"I know it does. But does it make things happen nicer the next time you run into that person?"

"Well, maybe not."

"What do you think will happen the next time you run into that person?"

"They might call me a name again."

"If they do that, do you think they might get mad and call you another name or even hit you?"

"Hit me!!??? If they hit me, I'll hit them back!"

"Does calling names and hitting back make anything better?"

He looks down at the floor again and I can barely hear him say, "Noooo."

"Listen, Puppers. I had a really nice friend one time. Then one day, I got angry at something she said when she called me a name.

"I really felt bad when I called her a name in return. We said we were sorry and we stayed friends. But then, on another day, she did something I didn't like. She called another friend of mine a name. I never saw my first friend again. She had turned into what I call a fiend.

"What's a 'fiend', Mama?"

"It is ONE LETTER away from being a f . . R . .iend, Puppers. Look at what I'm writing on this paper. I wrote the word 'FRIEND.' Now I'm writing again. Only this time, I'm leaving out the letter "R" in that word. That makes this word read FIEND.

"Puppers, a true FRIEND will have the letter 'R' in that word. To me, that *R* stands for ***RESPECT*** for the person I am talking with. And if someone is not acting like a true FRIEND, they will be a FIEND to you. A FIEND is someone who will not be nice and they won't respect you. Do you want to be a FRIEND or a FIEND?"

"I want to be a friend! So, you mean when I call names or hit someone, I'm being a FIEND?"

"That's exactly what I mean, Puppers. Did you like it when you got called that name?"

"No, I didn't."

"So you called a name back and that is when you turned into a

FIEND instead of a FRIEND."

"Oh, I get it. If I want to keep my FRIENDS, then I need to not be a FIEND."

"That's right! Remember that letter R to help you learn that you need to respect other people and your friends."

"Mama, what happens if the other person wants to be a FIEND?"

"Well, Puppers, all you can do is pray and ask God to help them. Then you can just continue trying to be a FRIEND instead of a FIEND. Okay?"

"Riiiiight, Mama. I gots it now!"

Oh, My Aching…!!!

"Look at me, Mama! I can really run, huh!!"

"Yes, Puppers! Look at you go!"

I have some empathy for Puppers. He also had seizures. He has some of what they call *residual effects* from them. This can mean his tongue is no longer perfectly centered in his mouth and when he runs, he runs sideways at times. However, he CAN still run fast. And I believe, at least in *his* mind, he pictures himself running as fast as any greyhound in the world!

Is he suffering? In some ways, he might feel the aches and pains. Especially when he is finished with the seizure, because his muscles tense up. But in most ways, I think he is oblivious to pain or at least not expressing it.

Suffering comes to all of us; even to animals. However, humans have the ability to know it, feel it, analyze it, and even hate it. Worst of all, we continue to ask that age-old question of, "Why me?"

I think I pretty much stopped asking that question about two years ago. In my younger days, because I had sooooooooo much I thought I could accomplish, I asked it all the time. Now, I still have a lot I think I can accomplish, but I'm older and perhaps a bit wiser.

I've been reading a lot of things lately that tell us why we suffer, or the possible reasons. I gloss over them now for the ONE reason that it simply doesn't matter anymore. What matters is that God is in charge and . . . I trust him.

Maybe that is how it is with Puppers and WE just don't know

it. Maybe, in his finite mind, he realizes that it just simply does not matter WHY we suffer.

Maybe he knows a lot more and a lot sooner than we do that God is simply, lovingly and powerfully, in charge of everything.

People don't want to believe that God loves us when we suffer or when others suffer. Yet, I do believe that. I believe God hurts right along with us. I can't SEE a lot of comfort in that thought, but just REALIZING He is there with me through it all is where I find my comfort and my courage to go on.

THAT is being "rooted in Him." That is like Puppers being focused on some trees to see if he can spot the raccoon we both saw last night. THAT was thrilling for him, just as being "rooted" in God is for me.

I guess I'm repeating what has been said so many times in so many ways. If we remain rooted in our Lord, then we need not ask WHY anymore. We just come to acceptance, have faith in the unseen and the unknown, be empathetic, and loving. Pain does build character and patience and love.

"Oh, my aching . . . !" becomes "My Lord and my God!". It will make believers out of us all as our faith blooms.

Leaning Trust

Puppers has shown me so much that I thought I would never learn it all. It only makes me believe with more intensity that God uses people and other ways to teach us about Himself.

The other day, I was leaning back in the chair and Puppers was laying lengthwise on my torso area. All of a sudden, his head went slack to the left and I discovered that he was . . . sound asleep!

The next afternoon, we took a nap together, as usual, and he was at the foot of the bed. Sometimes he sleeps right next to me, curled up near my legs or torso.

That night, he was curled up next to the back of my legs. I was in a somewhat twilight sleep when I turned over and curled up my knees. To my horror, he rolled off the bed onto the floor. I heard a loud THUD.

I sat bolt upright groping for the light. I turned it on and found him in a cowering position with a verrrrrry confused look on his face. It was as if he was saying, "What in the WORLD did I do to YOU!!"

I carefully picked him up and was quite surprised that he didn't run from me. I checked him from head to toe, bending all feet, legs, head . . . everything. He started a little nipping as if he thought I was playing with him.

All the time I'm checking him, I'm praying to Jesus that he is not hurt. I pick him up in my arms, and the tears of gratitude that he seemed okay began to flow. He kissed me like crazy as I told him how sorry I was, and that it was an accident.

He understood it was an accident.

He hopped out of my arms and down onto the bed, began wagging his tail and running all over the bed, then down onto his hassock and off running through the house. I knew then that he was okay . . . both physically, mentally, and yes, I believe spiritually, also.

You see, all animals no matter how small, know positively WHO their Creator is. And this seems to somehow carry over into the work they do on this earth, whether it is an ant colony or a cute puppy kissing me.

Today, after his fall from the bed, he again went to sleep with me while we were sitting in the chair . . . totally relaxed . . . leaning into what he knows to be loving, caring, compassionate arms.

I call it *leaning trust*. I think Puppers would call it the same thing. He wants me to ask you a personal question. How is YOUR *leaning trust* in Jesus today?

We both hope it is strong . . . lean into the One Who will hold you tightly when no one else is around or will do so.

Snackle

I had to be very quiet 'cause I was on the bed and Mama was still asleep. I had my head and front paws on her shoulder, and I was real still 'cause I don't know how long big people sleep. It sure seemed like a long time, though.

I was thinkin 'bout what I saw yesterday. You know, that thing Mama called *snow*. It sure felt funny to walk on it. My paws got all cold. But I just couldn't seem to make myself get off that snow.

I was hopin' Mama would wake up soon so I could look out the window and see if it was still there. Oh, oh, she's movin' on the bed. I like it when Mama wakes up. If I put my face in front of hers now, she will say, "'Good mornin', Puppers!" That is when we get time to let me give her a kiss, a cuddle, and sometimes to play a little bit.

I gave her a quick kiss this morning because I just HAD to get outside! I almost changed my mind when I heard a loud noise from out in the backyard!

"Mama, get up! Did you hear that? Did you hear it? There it goes again! What is that!!??"

"Well, Puppers, let's go see."

"No, Mama. I'm scared! It sounds awful. I'm afraid to go out there!"

She opened the curtain and then that awful, horrible noise came again. I ran to hide under the living room table.

"Come on, Puppers, it's okay."

Usually when Mama says that, I come right away, but not THIS time. All I could do was whine and stay under that table. Mama came over to pick me up. Oh, no! She's going to take me outside! We got out the door and I just leaned into her arms as I heard that noise again and something from the roof fell to the ground.

"What is it, Mama? Don't let go! I don't like snow anymore!"

"Puppers, that was just a piece of ice that came off the roof. The rain was freezing last night and it made ice on the roof and on the ground. See? It isn't anything to be afraid of and you can always walk on the grass over here."

"I don't know, Mama. It makes a bad sound. It sort of sounds like it's sayin', *Snackle!!*"

"Well, Puppers, I think you're right. When snow and ice fall apart, I guess we could call the snow and ice crakle a *snackle*. But that isn't any reason to be afraid. You know that Jesus made the snow and ice. He wouldn't make anything that pretty or loud so it would hurt us."

She is going to put me down on the ground now. Oh, boy, I'm not so sure about this. Maybe it will be okay if I just don't think about how I was sinking in the snow yesterday 'cause it was so deep. Each time I sank, though, Mama would come over and help me get up on my feet again. Here goes nothin', but I'm gonna keep my eyes on her!

"Wow! Mama, I'm not sinking anymore! Whee! This is great! Ooops! I slid a little faster than I wanted to slide!"

"That's okay, Puppers. Sometimes we just have to practice how to walk on snow and ice. We might slide. But if we practice not being afraid and trusting Jesus is with us all the time looking out for us, then we can learn how to walk on the slippery sides and let Him pick us up if we fall. That's what forgiveness means. And when He picks us up by forgiving us, then we need to practice where to walk the right way."

"Oh, I get it now, Mama. But what about the *snackle*?"

"Puppers, when we practice what I told you, we don't even have to worry about the *snackles* in life that we see or hear. We just turn to look at Jesus and He will make all the *snackle noises* go away or sound beautiful. Just listen now. Doesn't it sound prettier than before when we first came outside?"

"Yeah, Mama. Snow, ice and *snackles* is a lot of fun. Wanna play outside for a little while? At least until I have to go inside to get my toes warm."

Well, we did play a little while and we heard a lot more of those *snackles*, but I'm not as afraid now. Maybe the snackles and the ice will be around tomorrow and I can get in some more practice.

How 'bout you? Are you practicin'?

AAAGH!!! IT'S RAINING!!!

Shhh! Mama's sleepin'. I'm tryin' to be quiet, 'cause I was 'sposed to be takin' a nap, too!

Mama left the window drapes open so's I can see outside. It sure is rainin' out there. I don't mind the rain if it ain't too much. I get's outside and if it's a LOT of rain, it hits me on the head. And that hurts, 'cause I'm just a little guy.

Mamas' auntie gave me a yellow rain coat to wear. But I still can't get used to it. I feel like a sunflower in it and sometimes the big boys laugh at me. Mama says just to ignore them 'cause they aren't blessed like me to have a raincoat. I tries to ignore 'em, but it sure is hard. First, I has to try and pretend the rain ain't so hard on my head and then I has to try to ignore them. THEN, I has to remember that Jesus has blessed me with the raincoat that looks like a big sunflower!

That's an AWFUL lot for a little guy like me to 'member, don'tja think?

Anyway, when it rains harder, I don't get to go out and play as much on my Cadillac convertible. I has to stay indoors and try to get my *babies* to play with me in the nursery. I'm doin' that today, but I was thinkin' about somethin'. Why does God allow so much rain???? Aaaaagh! Sometimes, it just drives me crazy. I know what Mama would say, though.

Mama's up now. I'm going to ask her why!

"Now, Puppers. Listen. God lets a lot of rain fall in our lives and He never said we had to like it. What He does say is that we need to make the best of it. You know, find something positive to think about when the rain comes falling down. Like you. You can play in a warm home. You don't have to play outside or live outside like some of your friends. You have a neato raincoat to wear to help keep you dry when you DO get out. I know what, Puppers! Try to think of your raincoat like it is God's tank! It covers you and keeps you warm and dry. It also has a hood that helps you to block out all the teasing you get about it.

"Just remember, if you can think about all the positive things that happen when the rain falls in your life, then you can be JOY-FUL about all of it. God means it all to happen for His glory and for your good. Now, I know that is hard to understand when it is raining really hard. But just look around and see what the rain does. It makes things greeeeen! Yes! And if it is gonna make things green, then it will make you happier if you think about what God is doing when He lets it rain so hard!"

"Okay, Mama, I'll try but I still likes sunshine better!"

"I know, Puppers, but just think. When it stops raining and the sun comes out, there are TWO THINGS you can be happy about and thankful for!"

"Yeah! I gots two things to be happy about and some peoples don't, do they? Maybe next time them guys tease me, I'll just try to tell 'em that it is rainin' ***hard words***. But it don't bother me 'cause I knows the rain will stop soon and out comes the sun!!!"

"Yes, Puppers, the SON always comes out again. That is really good news, huh?!"

Uncle Doctors and Peanut Butter

Sometimes people are funny to watch. But not today. I got to go on the big bus and see Mama's doctor. I could tell even with Mama smilin' that this was NOT gonna be fun or funny. You see, Mama hurt her back and was gonna see uncle Dr. Jim. He helps her with her back, but sometimes it hurts when he does it. She smiles and yet I still see some itty-bitty tears come from her eyes.

Mama says that lots of people go to see their doctors and that they have a lot more wrong with them than she has. But I don't think that is totally true. 'Cause I've seen Mama tell aunt Dr. Dee on the phone that a LOT of things hurt her. Like her back or her legs or her head and sometimes her soul hurts her, too.

I think the only thing I can do is to get in Mama's arms and kiss her to let her know how much I love her.

I also think that when little kids has to go to THEIR uncle Doctors, that THEIR mama and daddy ought to hold them, love them, and cuddle them, too.

That happened to me last week. I got verrrry sick and Mama was really worried. So, I had to go see uncle Dr. Roy. I got on the big bus, but it wasn't as much fun this time, 'cause I was sick. I still got to see the big trucks and a squirrel, though.

My uncle Dr. Roy told me I had to get me some medi . . . uhm-mmm, how does you spell that big word, Mama? Oh . . . medicine. Medicine is pills.

Uncle Dr. Roy looked at me. He tried to look in my ears, but I wouldn't let him. He just checked me as best he could, but the neat

"

part is that I was less scared, 'cause Mama was holdin' me.

Then I got to go for a little walk. We got on the big bus again, but I still didn't feel too good. When we got home, Mama picked me up and put me on her lap. She got something in a big jar. It was my favorite! Peanut butter!!! Yay!! I must be gonna get a treat for bein' a good boy on the big bus!

Oops! What is that stuff she just put in the jar??

Hmmm . . . well, I likes the taste of peanut butter a lot, so I'll give it a try. Oh, oh! Mama put my medicine in the peanut butter. But you know, that is okay. 'Cause sometimes pills can taste nasty, huh? I didn't hardly taste them at all and that peanut butter sure tasted good!! I guess it was about an hour later and I started to feel really good! I got my bear and my bone, and went out in the back-yard to play.

Mama came out to check on me and was laughing hard 'cause she was so happy to see I was feelin' better. Then she said a little prayer. Honest! I heard her. She was thankin' Jesus that I was better.

Guess what I'm tryin' to tell you is that all of us need to have someone to help us when we gets sick. For instance, I know Mama and my uncle Doctors will help me. I help Mama by kissin' her and lettin' her know when she is about to have a seizure and if she is not feelin' good. I lay down on the bed with her and be reaaallly quiet so she can rest.

The other thing that Mama tells me is, "No matter what, Puppers. We both know that we can take care of each other. But we always need to remember that Jesus is right there with us and holding us both in His loving, merciful arms."

Now, I know what love is. But I'm not too sure what *merciful* means. Maybe it just simply means that we care about each other and we are kind to each other when we is sick and when we is well, hmmmm?

What does you think? Think maybe we ought to ALL try to do a itty-bitty bit more of that?? It is sort of like havin' good peanut butter (Yummmm!) and good uncle doctors and that means Jesus holds us when we is holdin' others. Mama calls that a big word and I will let her spell it for you . . . it is called COMPASSION.

So, I'm going to go play now and if I see someone who needs that big word or the word merciful, I will go do it. I hope you do, too!

'Spect

"Mama! Comere a minute, will ya?"

"What's up, Puppers?"

"Mama, what does *'spect* mean?"

"Spect? Hmmm . . . I'm not sure what word you're saying, Puppers. Do you mean like a little speck of dust?"

"Noooo. I meant like the other day when I laughed at someone and they says, 'You should have a little more 'spect' for other people.'"

"Oh, you mean *respect!* Well, let me see how I can explain this. Remember I told you that we don't tease people, Puppers, because that isn't nice?"

"Yeah. Like when the big boys tease me about being such a little guy or about my yellow raincoat."

"Yes! That isn't funny, is it? They left and it hurt your feelings!"

"Yeah!"

"Well, respect is when you don't laugh at people or the things they do when they are really trying to be helpful to others. You don't laugh at their homes or their clothes or how they talk or how they look. It's that sort of thing.

"Now, I'll give you an example. Your Mama has too much weight on her and sometimes people laugh at her. Your Mama doesn't wear fancy clothes. I wear clothes that are comfortable and keep me warm in the winter and cool in the summer.

"Do you understand what I mean? Respect means that you care about people and you love them for who they are."

"But, Mama, what if theys doing something naughty or mean, like stealing something?"

"Puppers, you still respect them because they are God's children and He still loves them. So, you should love them also. It doesn't mean that you like the things they have done, like stealing. But you still show them respect and love by praying for them and asking God to help them with their naughty problem.

"You might want to pray for me to help me lose some weight or pray for that little boy over there who is in a wheelchair. It isn't naughty for me to be overweight or for him to be in a wheelchair. You could pray that I could lose some weight so I could be healthier and you could pray that God will help him not be in so much pain in his wheelchair or that he would still have good, happy times while he has to use that wheelchair. Respect is just like love, Puppers."

"Even when they laughs at you, you still gots to respect them, Mama?"

"Yes, Puppers. You don't laugh at them. You just show them the love Jesus has inside of you for them. It takes some practice, but you can do it."

"Mama, is Jesus angry 'cause I laughed at that person?"

"Puppers, Jesus doesn't LIKE it when we do things like that. He made that person as His child. He still loves you AND that person, no matter what!"

"So, 'spect means *love*?"

"Yes, Puppers. You see, you cannot touch or see *love*, so respect is the way that we can SHOW someone we love them."

"Wow! So if I love someone, then I show them I respects them by bein' nice to them when I talks with them?"

"Yes, and it also means that you show them love by being kind to them, not laughing at them even if your other friends laugh."

"But, Mama, if my friends laugh and I don't laugh, then my friends won't like me anymore!"

"Sometimes, Puppers, you need to try to speak up and tell your friends that something is not nice to do. If they don't want to be your friends anymore, and I know that hurts, but you have a lot of other people in the world who WOULD like to be your friend because . . . you show love and respect."

"I get it. I need to think of love and *'spect* FIRST and THEN friends come around."

"Yes, then friends, like Jesus, come around and they will love and 'spect' you just like you love and *respect* them."

"Oooh! Mama! There is that person I laughed at and I want to go tell them I'm sorry. Can I do that right now?"

"Yes, Puppers. Hurry up and go to show some respect with an 'I'm sorry.'"

"Okay, Mama. Back in a minute!!!"

It Takes a Suddenly

Definition of **humble:** modest opinion of ones' own importance or rank . . . meekness . . . it removes pride.

When I watch Puppers on a daily basis, I don't see any pride in him. He is meek, gentle and compassionate. At times he can get angry. Especially if another dog tries to get on *his* Cadillac convertible scooter.

It makes me wonder how we get rid of pride and become more humble. I think the answer lies in LOOKING AT THE OTHER PERSON, whether it is an animal or human being.

When we look at the *other*, **we stop seeing ourselves.** We look at people and **SUDDENLY** try to shift gears to help them, talk with them, share with them, even learn to love them if they are our enemies. The focus is NOT on the *I* part of ***pride***.

We can get PRIDE and SELF-ESTEEM mixed up, also. We can learn the difference with the help of Jesus. Self esteem is STILL a focus on us. But it has a major component of having done something for someone else FIRST and then realizing **_we_** truly needed help to do that, whereas PRIDE stands alone . . . WE **stand alone** and **stand out** alone when we have PRIDE.

Also, notice the word **suddenly** . . . we switch gears suddenly. Just as quickly as St. Peter switched from being a stalwart defender of Jesus to denying Him instead. His **initial** prideful comments that he would die for Jesus, however, devastated him and SUDDENLY, he realized what Christ was trying to tell him.

To paraphrase it, Peter would become more OTHER-directed

in his life from that point on . . . truly focused totally on Jesus and telling others about Him.

Sometimes, it takes a *suddenly* to make us humble. We can be successful in many things, large or small, but we need to realize when the praise comes our way, that we could NOT have done any of it without the help of Jesus. So there we have it . . . the final answers to a complex issue of learning to be humble . . . three short-step answers:

1. Focus on the OTHERS in our lives as we

2. Let Jesus lead us and look to Him for TOTAL dependence about everything and then

3. Allow yourself and others some self-esteem. It is intensely different from pride.

Self-esteem acknowledges that we DID do something neat, but the glory and all else go to our Lord.

I believe Puppers has the right idea instilled in him by example from human beings, and mostly by the Lord. All I had to do was watch Puppers' behavior to figure out what it means to be **suddenly** humble.

Lovin'

Mama Debb read some cool stuff from her Bible today . . . **Love is very patient** she said . . . I try to be this way and some days it helps Mama. She worries a lot and I try to show her how not to do that. I sit on my hassock by the window, like I'm doing right now, and I just wait for her to have time to play with me. Now why would I just sit there for 2 hours? 'Cause the reward of gettin' to play with her is worth waitin' for. So I focus on the good that will come out of bein' patient.

Oh, yes. There are times when I wants to go, go, go. 'Specially when she tells me that we are going bye-bye. Bye-bye is a verrrrry special time for me! I hops from foot to foot and run around the house until she is ready. But the diff'rence in sittin' and runnin' **is in how you look at it.**

When you sits and waits, like *waitin' on God* as Mama Debb says, then you just keep a positive mind. And I think about how much I love Mama while I waits. Gettin' to go bye-bye is diff'rent because it MIGHT LOOK like I am bein' impatient when I runs around. But that is not what it is . . . it is EXCITEMENT!

Love is never boastful or proud . . . Mama is always talkin' about the *I* in pride. She tells me it is the worst thing that can happen to anybody. She praises me a lot when I does the right things. I gets a little proud. But if I thinks about it long enough, she is just givin' me compliments to show she loves me. Yes, sometimes I does some things bad. But she don't get angry with **_me_**. She gets upset with **_what I've done!_** This helps me to see there is a diff'rence between pride and self-esteem.

Mama is tryin' to show me that pride is totally selfish.

Self-esteem is just simply feelin' good about what you do for others . . . that's right . . . for OTHERS!

Love does not demand its' own way . . . This is like when we look only at ourselves with the pride thing. And we want what WE want NOW. We're not patient. If we demand our own way and get it, then we get that pride thing in there that WE won something. And none of that is good at all.

Love goes on forever . . . The only way love can go on forever is if we do it **unconditionally.** (That's a big word Mama had to help me figger out.) If we do that, then love goes on forever and ever and ever. She says it is like when Jesus died and He left that empty tomb behind. We not only gets eternal life, but we gets it forever. In addition to that, she says, ___maybe the empty tomb is when we empty our hearts of thinking only about ourselves.___ When we do that we are doin' that unconditional love thing with no strings attached to our love. It's just like Jesus did. We also have **patient love, kind love, and no pride.** We look at things other peoples need instead of ourselves. We give ourselves to others through unconditional love. *Wow!! That Bible passage goes round and round and round in a full circle, don't it?*

How is YOUR love circle today? Mine is gonna be great!!

Simply....Love

"Dear Puppers, I'm so very sorry." He looks up at me and then looks down.

All I can do now is sigh . . . and hope.

Puppers has slept with me since he was eight months old. During the past three weeks, he has chosen to go and sleep in the rocking chair in the living room. I miss his closeness and his cuddling next to my leg in the bed. I miss being able to be awakened when he has a seizure so that I can comfort him when he comes out of it. I miss hearing the little whiny noises he makes. Or the muffled barks when he is dreaming. And, I miss . . . simply . . . him.

I don't know why he has chosen to sleep elsewhere. I only know that if I go sit on the bed, he will stay, but the minute I try to lay down next to him, unless I hold him there, he goes into the living room. I guess I'm taking this personally. So my friends tell me, "Just let the dog be a dog." It is the most difficult thing I am doing since I have never had children. I consider him to be my family and see him as almost human.

Human feelings are a lot of mixed emotions. One minute we feel this way and another minute we feel the opposite or differently. I find love to be one of the strangest emotions and one that isn't easily explained in our human terms.

There's a line from the book "Love Story." It says, "Love means never having to say you're sorry." I don't find that true all the time or even some of the time. Love is a complicated thing. To me, love means you WANT to say you're sorry, even if you are saying it a lot.

Love means you say you are sorry because you want to never repeat an action and you want the person, in this case Puppers, to forgive you. You also want that person to not only to forgive you, but to forget what has happened and move on in life.

However, love has a drawback . . . people don't always forget. And now Puppers seems to not want to forget that I've done something.

Something has happened that has made him not want to sleep on the bed anymore when I am in it. I become dizzy trying to figure out what that is. I know of two times when he was small that he rolled off the bed accidentally. But he managed to bring himself back on the bed and cuddle up right away.

"Whatever the reason, my dear Puppers, love **does** mean I want to say I'm sorry. Love means to make every effort to help you feel comfortable and loved. Love means I don't try to even gently coerce you to stay on the bed with me so you will feel safe and warm on cold nights.

Love means I want you to forgive AND forget whatever has happened and to move on into the future with me . . . with hope, a feeling of safety and most of all that unconditional love you have always given to me and that I want to give to you.

Thanks for helping me find the key . . . let God be in charge . . . showing us through His unconditional love of Jesus . . . showing us the way . . . showing us how to love, forgive and forget, even when we are confused and worried about what seems to be this thing called,

"SIMPLY LOVE" . . . . from Mama

MARILYN

I'd like to introduce you to Marilyn. She is the faithful friend of my neighbor, Ken.

Marilyn never got the chance to meet Puppers. However, she is only four years old and just as playful as Puppers. If she had met Puppers, I believe they would've gotten along very well. However, she is about five times his size. She wants to play with other dogs and people, always racing toward them and wagging her tail.

In one story of this book, I mentioned Puppers playing with Jaker's who was more his size. But when Puppers would get tired, he would run to my chair. He called that his "safety zone".

Everyone, including animals, need some sort of safety zone. It's a place they can go where they can feel safe and secure. With Puppers, it was a place he could go to rest from playing so hard.

Puppers would tell you that people need places to go for a safety zone.

In fact, he looked at me one day and said, "Mama, you need to take a rest. Let's go into your safety zone." He ran to the bed, hopped up on it and wagged his tail.

It's still amazing to me how animals can sense what we human beings need. So I joined Puppers on the bed. He said, "Mama, let's cuddle." We did that and both of us fell into a deep sleep.

I was resistant at first because there was so much that I needed to do. Yet Puppers was so persuasive with his body language that I just couldn't resist it any longer.

"Well, Mama, there is times when you need someone to help you do something. That day, you needed me to help you relax and just enjoy the time together. You know, Mama, if you doesn't do that, you would just fall on the floor. And then what would I do? I'm too little to pick you up. And I guess about all I could do would be to kiss you until you got up. Or just lay down beside you and sleep on the floor with you."

Puppers helped guide me through so many circumstances. He deserves a lot of credit for just simply being himself and for meeting my needs.

As much as Ken is trying to train Marilyn, I sure would hate to see her lose her *puppiness* because I know he enjoys her as much as I have enjoyed Puppers.

You can tell by the look on Ken's face that he is thrilled to have her and that she gives him a lot of comfort, like I did with Puppers. A lot of Ken's energy is chasing her around and trying to get her to obey his commands.

I think Marilyn is also good for me because I see a lot of Puppers qualities in her. They are both friendly, compassionate and bow their heads when they are scolded. In general, they're just plain fun to be around.

So, the next time you look at an animal, be considerate and watch their body language. You can learn so much from them. Not only about the animal, but about yourself.

I know that Puppers would tell you that. If nothing else he would shout, "Puppers talkin' here." And Marilyn would say, "You tell 'em, Puppers!" I also know that God wants us to listen to Him, Puppers, and Marilyn because they are His precious gifts to us.

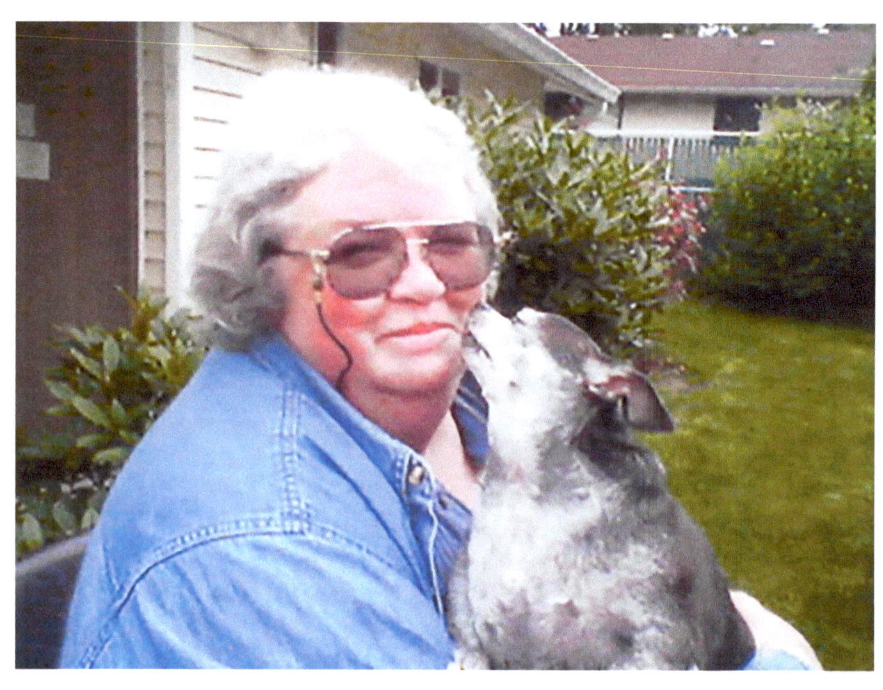

ABOUT THE AUTHOR

Deborah (Debb) Snyder was a former counselor and teacher. She graduated from Concordia College in 1982 so she could begin teaching at a private school in Inglewood, California.

Since her retirement, she has published numerous Christian articles. For twenty-eight years she has written The Son Brightener, a monthly newsletter sent to homebound members of her church, plus her friends and family. She is compiling these articles into three books that she hopes to publish. In addition, she is nearly finished with a Language Arts series that helps teachers learn to teach reading through phonics. Her dream is to get this massive series into all public schools in the U.S. and other countries.

Many of her ideas and editing for this book, other books and her articles came from her Christian friend and manager, Don Sullivan.

She currently resides in Vancouver, WA and is still working on more books.

GOD BLESS ALL OF YOU!

From Puppers and Mama Debb

For further information about the author,
her agent or the publisher, please contact
info@wanderingstream.org